PZ
7
.F26
B6

PZ7.F26B6

A041107601

SENECA
SHEPPARD
COLLEGE LIBRARY

SENECA
NEWNHAM
COLLEGE LIBRARY

Date Due			
MAR 1 4 1977	FEB - 8 1996		
DEC 5 1977	Apr. 15/96.		
DEC 1 2 1977			
MAR 2 6 1979			
OCT 1 5 1986			
FEB 0 3 1987			
FEB 1 1 1991			
MAR 2 0 1991			
FEB - 6 1992			
NOV 0 2 1993			

PROPERTY OF
SENECA COLLEGE
LIBRARY

SENECA
NEWNHAM
COLLEGE LIBRARY

WITHDRAWN

SHEPPARD
COLLEGE LIBRARY

172

The Boy With A Problem

by Joan Fassler

illustrated by Stuart Kranz

Behavioral Publications, Inc.
New York

CHILDREN'S SERIES ON PSYCHOLOGICALLY RELEVANT THEMES

Titles

by Joan Fassler, Ph.D.   ALL ALONE WITH DADDY

THE MAN OF THE HOUSE

ONE LITTLE GIRL

MY GRANDPA DIED TODAY

THE BOY WITH A PROBLEM

DON'T WORRY, DEAR

by Terry Berger   I HAVE FEELINGS

Review Committee:

Leonard S. Blackman, Ph.D.
Teachers College, Columbia University

Gerald Caplan, M.D.
Harvard Medical School

Eli M. Bower, Ed.D.
National Institute of
Mental Health

Series Editor:
Sheldon R. Roen, Ph.D.
Teachers College, Columbia University

Copyright© 1971 by Behavioral Publications, Inc.

All rights reserved. Except for use in a review, the reproduction or utilization of this work in any form or by any electronic, mechanical, or other means, now known or hereafter invented, including photocopying and recording, and in any information storage and retrieval system is forbidden without the written permission of the publisher.

Manufactured in the United States of America
Library of Congress Catalog Card Number

78-147125

This book is dedicated to my husband,
Leonard Fassler, who always takes the time to listen.

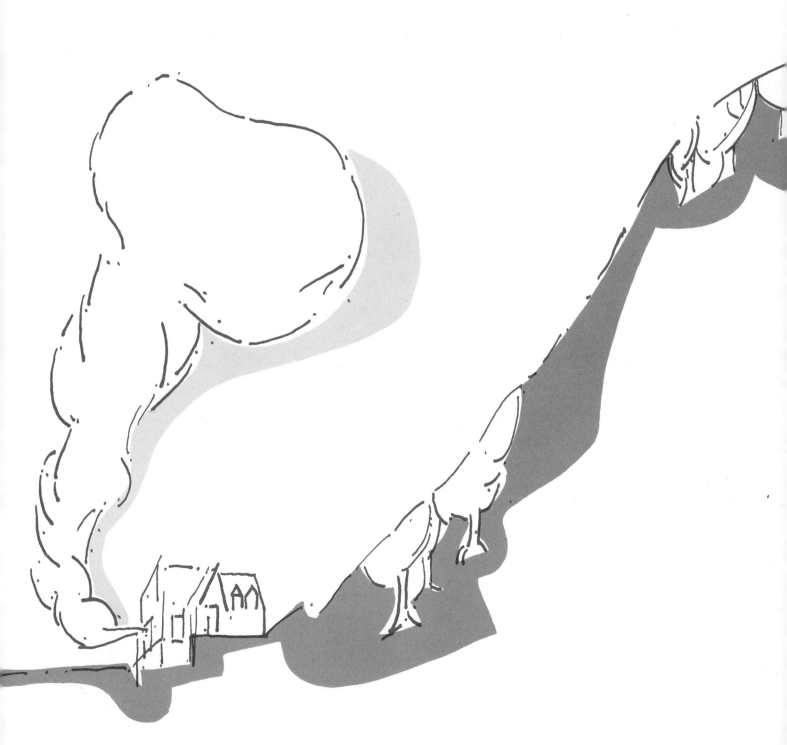

At the bottom of a very big hill sat a little red house. And inside this house lived a boy named Johnny. And Johnny was a boy with a problem.

Johnny's problem bothered him all day and all night. In the morning he could hardly eat his breakfast because the problem was so big that he couldn't swallow his food. And at night he couldn't fall asleep for a long, long time because the problem kept spinning round and round in his head. And in school he could hardly do his work because he was always thinking about his problem.

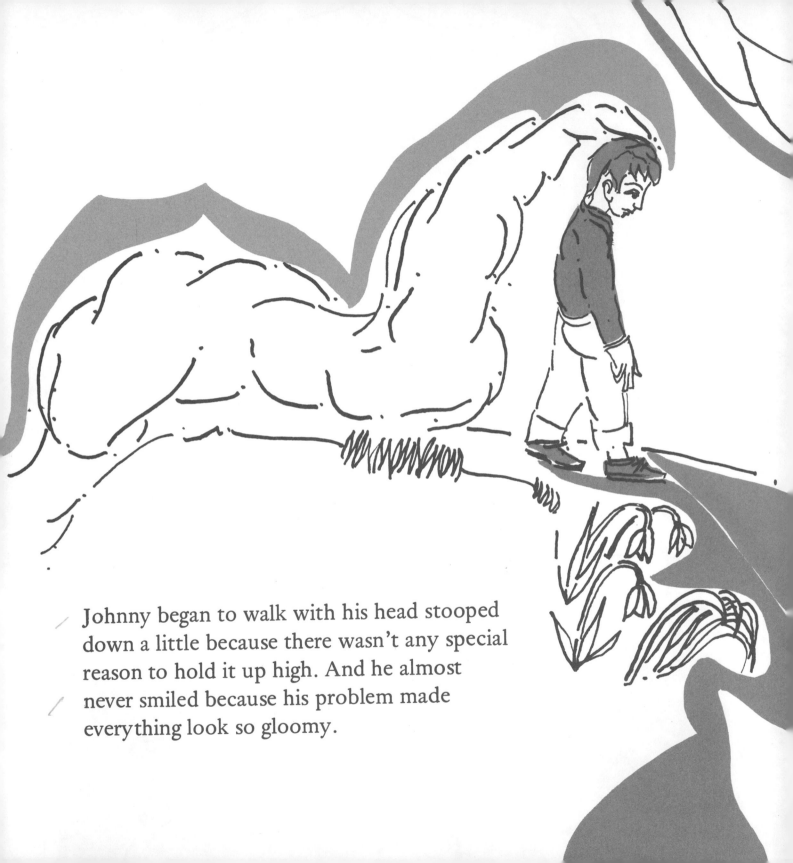

Johnny began to walk with his head stooped down a little because there wasn't any special reason to hold it up high. And he almost never smiled because his problem made everything look so gloomy.

Sometimes Johnny's problem even gave him
tummyaches — the little rumbly kind of
tummyaches that made him wonder every
now and then if he was going to have to spit
up right there in the middle of everything.

And, most days, when school was out,
Johnny didn't even feel like playing
. . . because nothing seemed like fun.

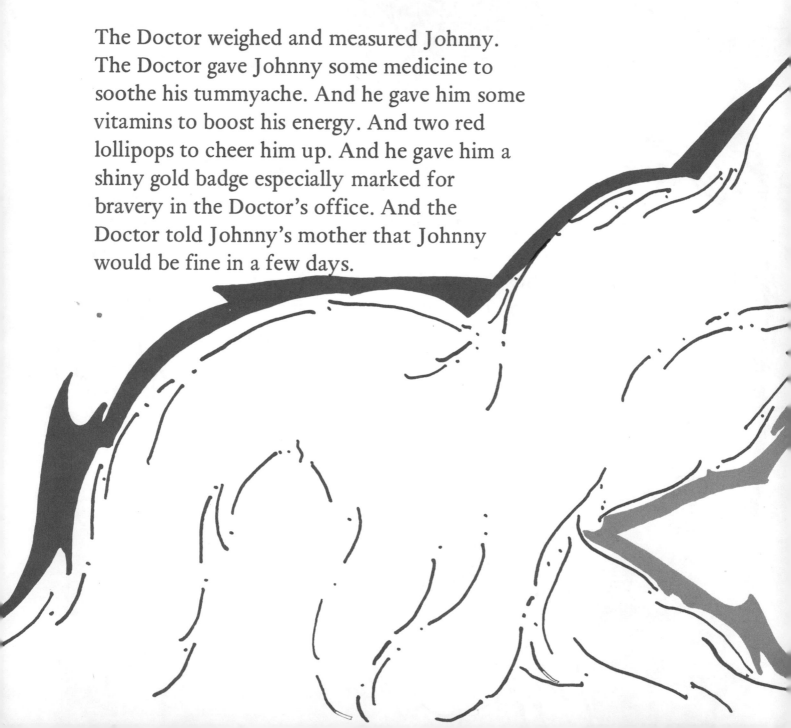

Johnny's mother knew that Johnny didn't
feel well. So she took Johnny to the Doctor.

The Doctor weighed and measured Johnny.
The Doctor gave Johnny some medicine to
soothe his tummyache. And he gave him some
vitamins to boost his energy. And two red
lollipops to cheer him up. And he gave him a
shiny gold badge especially marked for
bravery in the Doctor's office. And the
Doctor told Johnny's mother that Johnny
would be fine in a few days.

Johnny didn't especially feel like sucking the two red lollipops. And he didn't feel like wearing the shiny gold badge either. But he did take the medicine. And he did take the vitamins. And he hoped he would start feeling better soon.

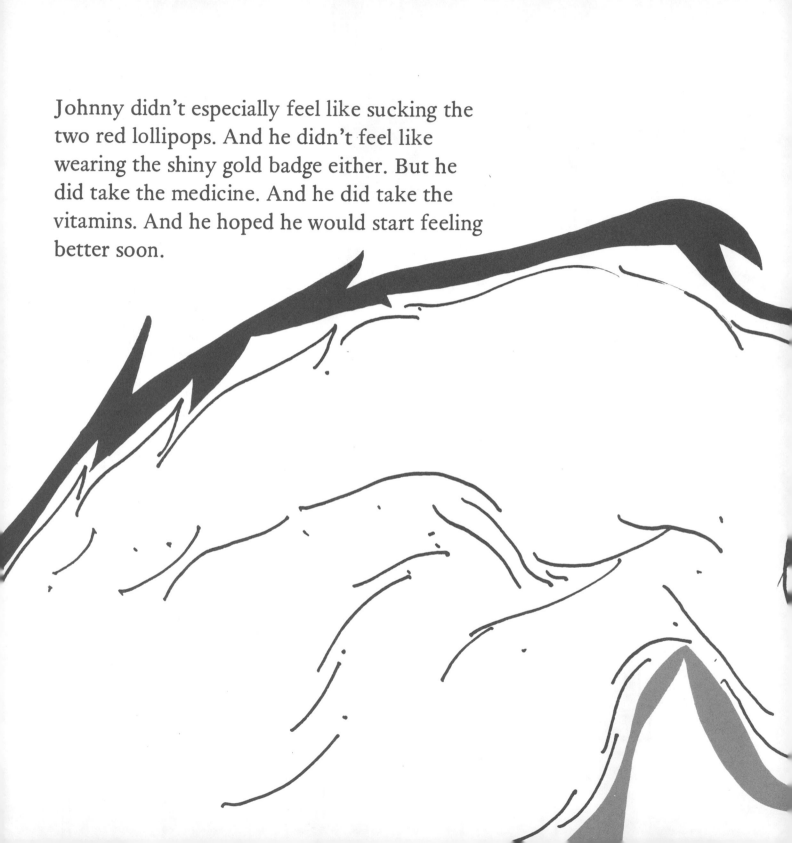

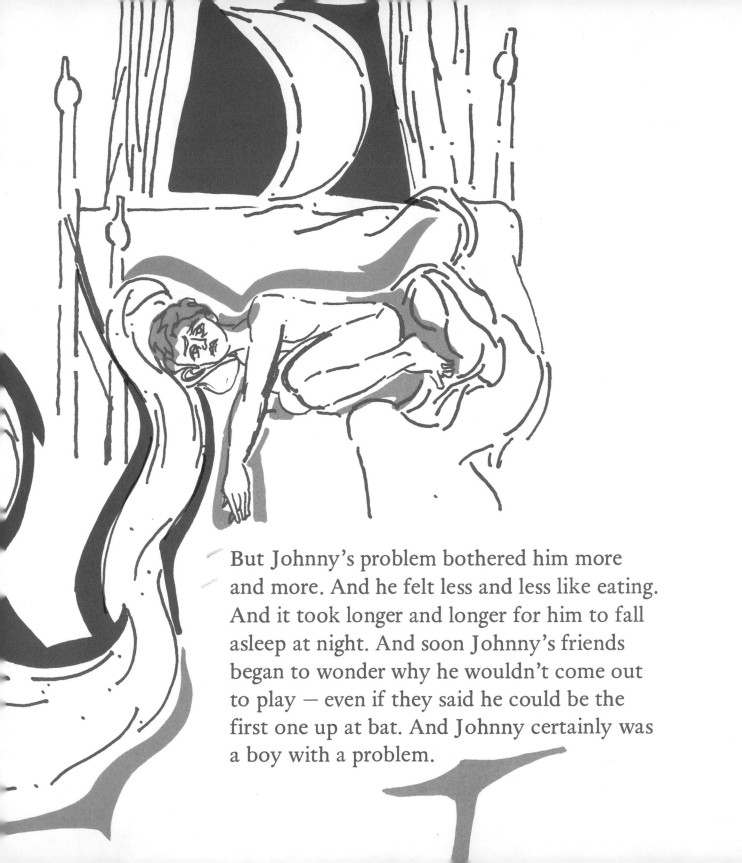

But Johnny's problem bothered him more and more. And he felt less and less like eating. And it took longer and longer for him to fall asleep at night. And soon Johnny's friends began to wonder why he wouldn't come out to play — even if they said he could be the first one up at bat. And Johnny certainly was a boy with a problem.

One day Johnny wanted to tell his mother
about his problem. Just as he tried to explain
the whole thing to her, his mother interrupted
him. "Little boys shouldn't have so many
worries," said his mother, as she patted
Johnny gently on the head. "Just forget all
about it and I am sure everything will be
fine." Johnny thought that maybe his mother
was right. So he took a deep breath and he
tried very hard to forget all about his
problem.

But he still had trouble swallowing his food.
And he still had trouble falling asleep at night.
And he still couldn't keep up with his work in
school. And the squishy rumbles in his
tummy grew bigger and bigger. And Johnny
was still a boy with a problem.

The next day Johnny decided to talk to his teacher. He waited after school. Then, very quietly, somewhat shyly, Johnny went up to her desk. And Johnny began to tell his teacher about his problem. Before he got very far, the teacher interrupted him. "I have a great idea," she said. "If you do just what I tell you, your problem won't bother you any more at all." And Johnny's teacher told Johnny exactly what to do.

Johnny tried to do what the teacher said. But
somehow it didn't really help at all. Johnny
still had trouble swallowing his food. And he
still had trouble falling asleep at night. And he
still didn't feel like playing with his friends.
And the squishy rumbles in his tummy grew
even bigger. And Johnny was still a boy with
a problem.

The next day Johnny's friend Peter knocked
at his door. "Hi," said Peter. "How about a
game of catch?" "No," said Johnny, "I don't
feel like playing ball." And he closed the
door. But Peter knocked again. "Come on out
anyway," Peter said. "We don't have to do
anything special if you don't want to." And
Johnny put on his jacket and went outside
with Peter.

"I don't see you around much any more," Peter said. And Johnny nodded his head. "I hardly come outside any more," he told his friend. "Why," asked Peter, "Is something the matter?" "Yes, there *is* something," Johnny said. "Something has been bothering me for a long time now." "Want to tell me about it?" said Peter in a quiet, gentle kind of voice. Johnny took a deep breath. "Okay," he said. But deep inside himself Johnny didn't really believe that Peter was going to be any help at all.

Then Johnny and Peter walked slowly up the big hill. And all the way up to the top of the hill Johnny told Peter about his problem. And Johnny and Peter turned around and walked slowly down the hill. And all the way down to the bottom of the hill Johnny told Peter about his problem.

And do you know what Peter did? He certainly didn't have any medicine to cure Johnny's problem. And he didn't pat Johnny on the head and tell him to forget all about his problem. And he didn't think of even one clever way to solve Johnny's problem.

No. Peter didn't do any of these things. But Peter did the most wonderful thing of all.

Peter listened! He listened in a very special, very serious way.

All the way up to the top of the hill, Peter
listened.

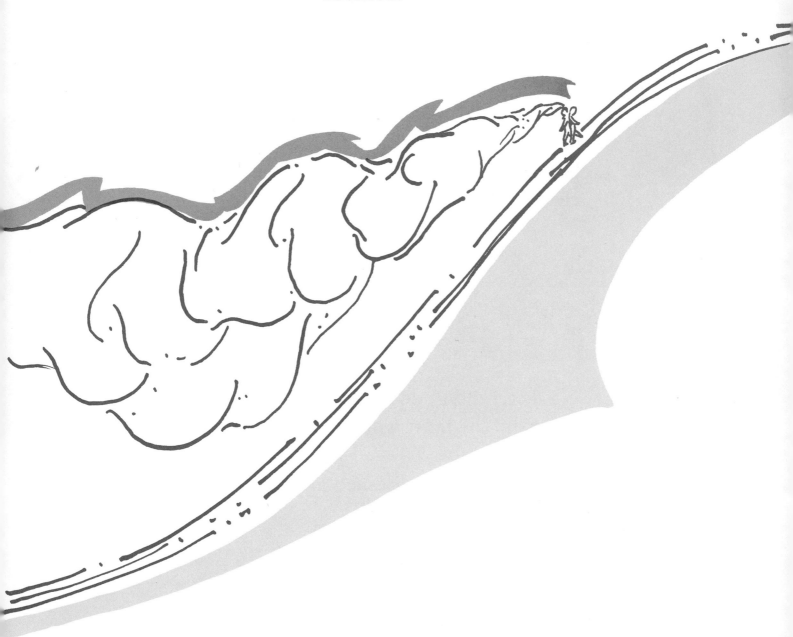

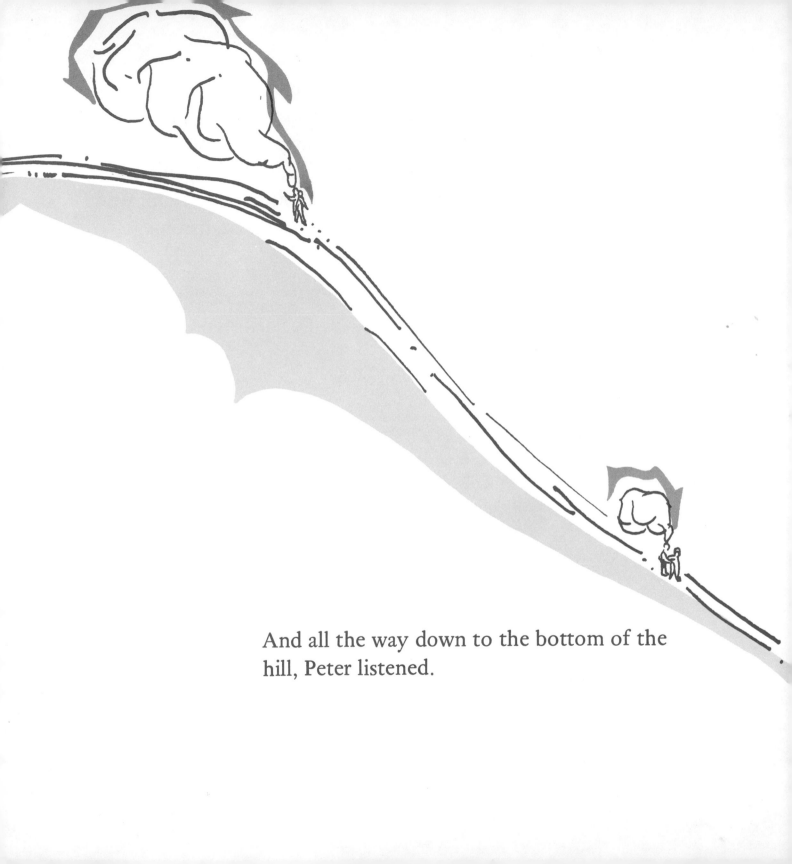

And all the way down to the bottom of the hill, Peter listened.

From the tip of his toes to the top of his head, Peter listened. He listened just as hard as he knew how to listen. He listened until Johnny had said absolutely everything that he could possibly say about his problem. And even then Peter went right on listening.

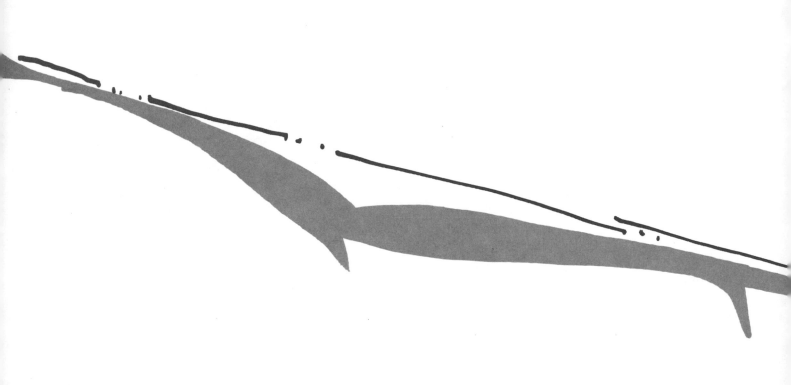

Until it began to get dark. "I think we better go home now," Peter said. "It's getting late." So Johnny and Peter walked together just a little bit more. Then Johnny went home to his house. And Peter went home to his house.

That night Johnny's dinner tasted better than any dinner he had eaten for days and days. And dessert was so good that Johnny asked for more.

Later Johnny felt tired, so he yawned and
stretched and went upstairs to bed. And the
fresh clean sheets on his bed felt good against
his body. And the big, soft blanket was warm
and cuddly. Soon Johnny turned over on his
side, curled himself up comfortably, and fell
fast asleep.

The next morning, Johnny woke up a little bit late and a whole lot hungry. Then he ate a big breakfast and hurried off to school.

And on that particular day, Johnny discovered that his school work wasn't so terribly hard after all. And, on that very same day, the rumbles in his tummy slowly disappeared.

Later, as he walked home from school,
Johnny noticed that the air smelled good.
And he noticed that the sky looked pretty.
Then Johnny saw some boys leaping and
laughing and tossing a ball around. Johnny
stood off on the side for a while and watched
them. And he held his head up high and
smiled because he felt so good inside.

And do you know what? Johnny didn't especially feel like a boy with a problem any more at all. Now he simply felt like a plain ordinary kind of boy who wanted to have some fun. So Johnny jumped up high to catch a ball that came whizzing his way.

And Johnny and the boys had a great catch together.

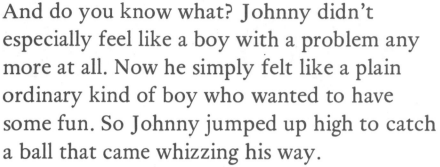